P9-DBP-254

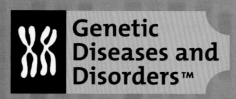

Genetic Diseases and Disorders™

Huntington's Disease

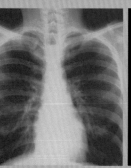
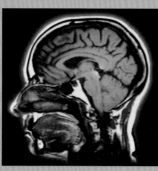
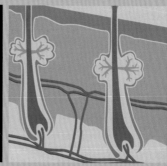
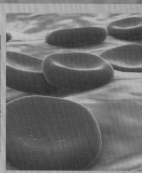

Johanna Knowles

L T 32725

The Rosen Publishing Group, Inc., New York

In memory of Woody Guthrie (1912–1967)

Published in 2007 by The Rosen Publishing Group, Inc.
29 East 21st Street, New York, NY 10010

Copyright © 2007 by The Rosen Publishing Group, Inc.

First Edition

All rights reserved. No part of this book may be reproduced in any form
without permission in writing from the publisher, except by a reviewer.

Library of Congress Cataloging-in-Publication Data

Knowles, Johanna.
Huntington's disease / Johanna Knowles.—1st ed.
      p. cm.—(Genetic diseases and disorders)
Includes bibliographical references.
ISBN 1-4042-0694-9 (library binding)
1. Huntington's chorea—Juvenile literature.
I. Title. II. Series.
RC394.H85K66 2007
616.8'3—dc22

                                                        2005028779

Manufactured in the United States of America

On the cover: Background: Nerve cells of the human cerebral cortex.
Foreground: Magnetic resonance image (MRI) of woman's head, side view.

Contents

Introduction 4

1 **The History of Huntington's Disease** 8

2 **Which Clues Will Lead to a Cure?** 17

3 **Symptoms, Diagnosis, and Treatment** 25

4 **Huntington's Disease Today** 35

5 **The Future of Huntington's Disease** 40

Timeline 52

Glossary 54

For More Information 56

For Further Reading 58

Bibliography 59

Index 62

Introduction

What would you do if you found out you had a 50 percent chance of developing a fatal disease? For people who have a parent with Huntington's disease, this question is all too real.

Huntington's disease (HD) causes nerve cells in certain areas of the brain to deteriorate. As this happens, it becomes harder to control thoughts, feelings, and movements. Eventually, the body becomes too weak to fight off other illnesses, leading to death. After a person first begins to develop symptoms of HD, he or she will usually live between ten and thirty more years before dying from complications related to the disease.

Although the cause of HD had been a mystery until recently, people have described the symptoms of the disease for a long time. In fact, descriptions of what researchers now believe to be symptoms of HD can be traced all the way back to the Middle Ages (around AD 500–1500). But it wasn't called Huntington's disease back then. The disease was first known as chorea, from the Greek word

This illustration shows a group of patients with senile chorea, a disease whose symptoms appear after age sixty. People with senile chorea suffer from sudden, jerking movements that give the impression of dancing. Some scientists believe senile chorea is a late form of Huntington's disease.

choreia, meaning "dance." You've probably heard of the English word "choreography" (dance composition), which comes from the same root. Chorea described how people with the disorder moved in an uncontrolled, dancelike motion.

The present-day name for the disease comes from George Huntington. He was a doctor from Long Island, New York, who described the disease in a medical journal in 1872. Like many researchers before him, Huntington noticed how HD symptoms appeared to run in families. HD is a genetic disease, meaning a person inherits the disease from a parent.

How do people know if they're at risk of developing HD? First, a person has to know if either of his or her biological (birth) parents has HD. If the answer is yes, the person has a 50 percent chance of inheriting the disease. Special blood tests can determine if the person has the defective gene that causes HD.

Other factors don't seem to play a role in whether a person will develop HD. For example, HD affects both men and women and is found in people of different races and ethnicities. According to the Huntington's Disease Association, about 1 in every 10,000 people in the United States has HD. Cases of HD have been found in every country of the world. In the United States today, there are approximately 30,000 cases of HD. Another 150,000 Americans have a 50 percent risk of developing the disease.

The early symptoms of HD vary from person to person. Physical, or "movement," symptoms can include mild clumsiness and muscle spasms. As the disease progresses, these symptoms increase. People with HD may also have trouble with their speech. For example, people with HD may notice that their speech becomes halting or slurred as the disease progresses. Some people with HD also have trouble swallowing.

HD symptoms also include emotional and cognitive problems, or difficulties involving thought and memory. For example, a person may have trouble learning new things or keeping information straight. In time, it may be harder and harder to remember or to pay attention.

Many people with HD also experience depression and mood swings. Sometimes it is hard to know if depression is a result from coping with the disease or a symptom of the disease. Either way, depression is a serious disorder that needs to be treated.

The age at which people develop symptoms of HD varies from person to person. Adult-onset HD (the most common type of HD) usually begins in middle age. Early-onset HD, which is also called juvenile HD, is less common. Juvenile HD develops in young people before age twenty. In general, the earlier the onset of the disease, the faster it tends to progress. But, in all cases, the fatal disease tends to last from ten to thirty years. Infections, such as pneumonia, are the most common causes of death.

What does the future look like for patients newly diagnosed with HD? Is it possible to find a cure? Many believe researchers are very close to finding a cure. As with all diseases, the more we learn about it, the closer we come to figuring out a way to prevent it.

1

Symptoms of Huntington's disease have been written about for a long time. In fact, way back in the sixteenth century, the Renaissance physician and alchemist Paracelsus (1493–1541) coined the term "chorea" to describe the uncoordinated movements of people with HD.

One hundred years later, in the 1630s, English colonists in Massachusetts used the term "Saint Vitus's dance" to describe the same type of movement. Saint Vitus was the patron saint of dancers. Not long after, in 1692, many people were accused of being possessed by the devil because of their uncontrolled body movements. About twenty were tried and sentenced to death in the famous witch trials in Salem, Massachusetts. Some historians now believe some of these people may have had HD.

In his writings, Paracelsus described three different types of choreas. Involuntary movement was a symptom common to all three types. Researchers now believe the disease he called "chorea naturalis" was Huntington's disease.

It wasn't until the 1840s that HD was first described in medical literature as "chronic hereditary chorea." At this time, three doctors—one in the United States, one in England, and one in Norway—each described, in separate accounts, the involuntary movements and mental disturbances of their patients. They also noted that these traits appeared to be inherited from a parent who displayed similar behavior. But the cause of HD and how to treat it remained a mystery.

Linking HD in Families

Finally, in 1872, a famous paper called "On Chorea" was published in the United States in the Philadelphia journal the *Medical and Surgical Reporter*. The paper was written by George Huntington. Huntington was an American doctor who described the symptoms of chorea in detail. Huntington based his paper on notes he took while observing his father's and

George Huntington was not the first person to document symptoms of HD. However, his description of the disease was so complete that his paper, "On Chorea," became very well known. The disease is still widely known by the name Huntington's chorea.

grandfather's patients. Both men were doctors who had noticed involuntary shaking in some of their patients. Huntington described how these symptoms were common in families, and he believed that the disease was inherited. In addition to physical symptoms, Huntington also noted the patients' mental decline. The careful observations and conclusions outlined in Huntington's paper helped spark widespread interest in the disease, which was eventually named after him.

It took many more years of research, however, before scientists were able to figure out what part of the brain was being affected by the disease. In 1910, researchers finally identified the parts of the brain that are the targets of cell death in patients with HD. These structures are the caudate nuclei. (A single one is called a caudate nucleus.)

Another key turning point in the study of HD occurred in 1953, when James Watson and Francis Crick discovered the structure of deoxyribonucleic acid (DNA). DNA is the key to our bodies' genetic makeup. The discovery of its structure

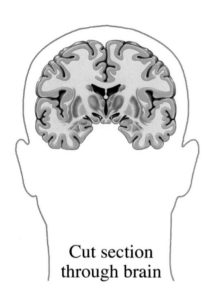

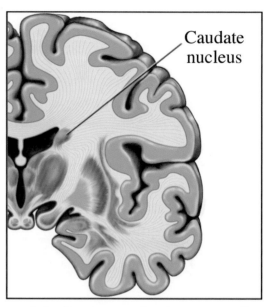

Caudate nucleus

Cut section through brain

The caudate nucleus is a part of the brain involved in controlling the body's movement and coordination. There is one caudate nucleus in each hemisphere of the brain. They are C-shaped structures with a wider head at the front, a body, and a tail at the bottom.

came at a time when there was a growing interest in human genetics. Many people accurately believed that learning about DNA was also the key to finding a cure to some genetic diseases. There was a surge in publications about HD, but the disease still remained a puzzling mystery. It was a mystery a growing number of people wanted to solve.

Research Leads to Discovery

In 1972, on the 100th anniversary of the publication of George Huntington's famous paper "On Chorea," HD researchers

THE WEXLER FAMILY MAKES A DIFFERENCE

Leonore Wexler was diagnosed with HD in 1968. Devastated by his wife's disease, her husband, Milton Wexler, was determined to learn more. He and his two daughters, Nancy and Alice, embarked on a search for a cure. Milton Wexler was a well-known psychologist. He worked hard to bring together world-renowned researchers to focus on HD research. He established the Foundation for Research in Hereditary Disease, which later became the Hereditary Disease Foundation. The foundation funds research and sponsors workshops where researchers can share information and ideas about HD.

Leonore Wexler's daughter Nancy played a key role in HD research as well. Like her father, Nancy Wexler wanted to encourage researchers to keep working to learn more about the disease. She led a team of scientists to Lake Maracaibo in Venezuela to study people who had HD. Why Venezuela? There is an unusually dense cluster of HD patients who live there.

Dr. Nancy Wexler began studying Venezuelans with HD in 1979. She gained the trust and friendship of many families by explaining that she was also at risk for the disease. Here she is pictured with one of the young people whose lives she hopes to improve through her research.

Some believe that because the area is so isolated, families who carry the gene continue to pass it down through generations. What makes the site a good place for HD research is that researchers can study a large group of people affected by the defective gene. The researchers collected blood samples from many HD patients. These samples helped lead to the discovery of a genetic marker for HD in 1983. (Genetic markers are specific genes in DNA that have a recognizable trait and can be used in family or population studies to track diseases.) Nancy Wexler also helped researchers map genes responsible for other diseases, including Alzheimer's disease, kidney cancer, and certain mental disorders. Today, Nancy Wexler is president of the Hereditary Disease Foundation.

Alice Wexler, Leonore Wexler's other daughter, has also contributed to the study of HD and HD awareness. She wrote the book *Mapping Fate: A Memoir of Family, Risk, and Genetic Research.* Leonore Wexler died in 1978.

held the International Centennial Symposium on Huntington's Disease. They got together to collect all the information known about HD up to that date. During that same year, Thomas L. Perry discovered lowered levels of GABA (gamma-aminobutyric acid) in the brains of HD patients. GABA is a hormone that regulates levels of dopamine in the brain. Dopamine is a chemical in the brain that helps regulate movement, balance, and walking. Lower levels of GABA weaken the motor system of the body and lead to the movement symptoms of HD. Many thought this could be a clue to how HD progressed.

In 1976, Joseph T. Coyle developed the first rat model of HD. Using rat models allows researchers to study the progression of diseases. Coyle inserted the chemical kainic acid into the brains of rats to cause damage to a specific area of the brain that controls movement, balance, and walking. After the injections, the rats began to exhibit HD-like symptoms including weight loss, uncontrolled movements, and brain damage. By carefully watching the symptoms progress in rats, researchers hoped to learn more about HD and eventually figure out how to control and even prevent its symptoms. The ultimate goal, of course, was to find a cure for HD.

All this research finally led the United States Congress to take action. In 1977, Congress approved the establishment of the Commission for the Control of Huntington's Disease. The purpose of the commission was to develop a comprehensive report on HD in the United States.

A major breakthrough occurred in 1983, when scientists discovered a gene marker linked to HD. This discovery led them to determine that the Huntington gene is located on a particular chromosome, which is a bundle of DNA and protein found in the cell nucleus. The Huntington gene is located on chromosome 4.

Discovering where the Huntington gene is located made it possible to figure out how likely it is for a person to inherit HD. Ten years after the general location was discovered, the Huntington gene was located at a more specific site on the chromosome: 4p16.3. This number is the identifier for the Huntington gene. The 4 stands for chromosome 4, the *p* indicates that it is located on the short arm of the chromosome, and the other numbers pinpoint the exact location on the chromosome where the gene is located. By isolating the gene to this specific location, researchers could then focus on how a defective version of the gene causes HD in the human body.

Some Diseases and Disorders Related to Chromosome 4

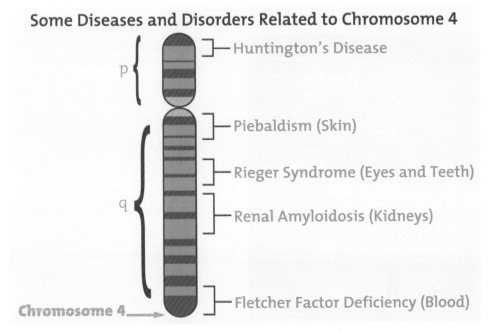

- Huntington's Disease
- Piebaldism (Skin)
- Rieger Syndrome (Eyes and Teeth)
- Renal Amyloidosis (Kidneys)
- Fletcher Factor Deficiency (Blood)

Chromosome 4

The gene responsible for Huntington's disease is located on the short arm (p) of chromosome 4. Genes related to diseases and disorders are located on the long arm (q) of the chromosome, as well. This image shows the approximate locations of the genes related to four other diseases and disorders, all rare.

Where We Are Now

Neurologists, psychologists, psychiatrists, and other scientists continue to study the symptoms and progression of HD in patients. They hope that by learning all they can, they will be able to develop new therapies. For example, using positron-emission tomography (PET), an advanced type of X-ray, scientists can see how the defective gene affects various structures in the brain and how it affects the body's chemistry and metabolism. The more accurately scientists can predict how HD will affect the body, the more effectively they can

CGATTCTGAACATGATACGTACTGGTCCACTAGAACTGAACTCGAGAGGTACTACAC

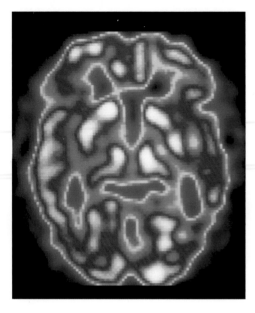

This is a PET scan showing a normal, healthy brain. PET stands for positron-emission tomography. PET scans help scientists measure chemical activity in different areas of the brain. They are a very useful medical tool for identifying neurological conditions like HD.

treat symptoms and figure out how to slow or stop the disease from progressing.

At the present time, medications can help treat specific symptoms of HD, such as depression. But there are still no proven treatments to help prevent the eventual physical and mental decline caused by the disease. This means that HD is still considered a fatal disease.

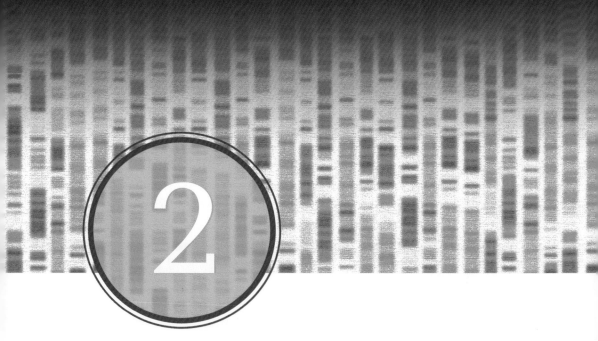

The discovery of the Huntington gene and where it is located is probably the biggest clue to the HD mystery. To start with, the 1983 discovery of genetic markers linked to HD made it possible to predict whether a person has inherited a faulty Huntington gene. Not all people at risk of HD want to learn if they have the faulty gene. For some people, however, getting treatment for symptoms as soon as they appear means having a better quality of life for a longer time.

But how can the latest advances in HD research bring scientists closer to more effective treatment—and maybe even a cure—for HD? This requires us to look more closely at the genetics of HD.

PIONEERING GENETIC RESEARCHERS AND LEADING EXPERTS ON HUNTINGTON'S DISEASE

Philippus Aureolus Theophrastus Bombast von Hohenheim (1493–1541)

Known simply as Paracelsus, this Swiss-born physician and notable alchemist and reformer during the Renaissance period introduced the name *chorea sancti viti* (Latin for "St. Vitus's dance") to describe what is now known as HD.

Gregor Mendel (1822–1884)

Mendel was a nineteenth-century monk who lived in Austria. He figured out some laws of genetic inheritance by growing, of all things, peas. Mendel planted lots of different varieties of peas in his monastery garden to observe the reproductive patterns of the flowering pea plants. By looking at the plants' traits (flower color, petal shape, etc.), he was able to make a connection of inheritance. Mendel discovered that during reproduction, each plant transmitted one copy of each gene to its offspring and that each gene pair was inherited independently. What Mendel didn't know was that genes are packaged on chromosomes. Mendel's studies eventually led to the field now known as genetics.

George Huntington (1850–1916)

At age twenty-two, this American physician submitted the now-famous paper "On Chorea" to the *Medical and Surgical Reporter.* Huntington was praised for his accurate and graphic descriptions of the symptoms associated with HD.

Nancy Wexler (1945–), James Gusella (1952–), Michael Conneally (1931–), and David Housman (1946–)

Nancy Wexler and her team of researchers have collected 18,000 blood samples from a group of people living in San Luis, Venezuela, a village on Lake Maracaibo. Here, an unusually high number of people are living with HD. After years of careful research and documentation, Wexler submitted cell cultures to Gusella, Conneally, and Housman to analyze the DNA. These samples led to the discovery of the exact location of the Huntington gene in 1993.

Understanding DNA

Whether a person will develop HD depends on his or her DNA. You have probably heard a lot about DNA in the media. Crime scene investigators on television often use it to solve cases. But what exactly is DNA, and what does it have to do with genetic diseases?

DNA stands for "deoxyribonucleic acid." Humans and other living organisms pass information to their offspring through DNA. When two people have a baby, DNA from each parent is the key ingredient passed on to the baby. It determines the baby's eye and hair color, skin color, and more. But DNA can also carry some unwanted traits, including genetic diseases like HD.

One helpful way to understand DNA is to think about the English language alphabet. We use twenty-six letters to form words. We then use these words to make sentences, which in turn help us to communicate. DNA has its own four-letter alphabet, or chemical code: A, C, G, and T. These are called

CGATTCTGAACATGATACGTACTGGTCCACTAGAACTGAACTCGAGAGGTACTAGA

Which physical traits did these children inherit from their mother? Some traits, such as facial features, are obvious. Other traits are more difficult to identify. One way to know if children have inherited certain genetic diseases from their parents is by comparing their DNA with their parents' DNA.

nucleotides, and each one represents a chemical, or base. Here is what the letters stand for:

A	=	adenine
C	=	cytosine
G	=	guanine
T	=	thymine

In the English language, words can be made up of just a few letters or many letters. But DNA words, or codes, are more uniform, with specific rules for how the letters are arranged. For example, A always pairs with T, and C always pairs with G. If you were to look at a DNA molecule, you would see what looks like a long, twisting ladder. This is called a double helix. Each rung of the "ladder" is made up of two paired nucleotide bases. Combinations of these pairs create a code that determines a gene's function. Human bodies have approximately 25,000 genes, and each of these genes provides information that contributes to an individual's characteristics.

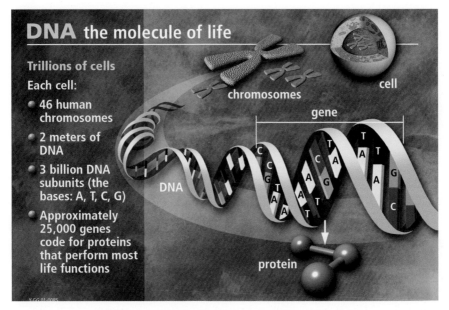

DNA the molecule of life

Trillions of cells

Each cell:
- 46 human chromosomes
- 2 meters of DNA
- 3 billion DNA subunits (the bases: A, T, C, G)
- Approximately 25,000 genes code for proteins that perform most life functions

chromosomes

cell

gene

DNA

protein

The first accurate model of a DNA molecule was proposed in 1953 by researchers James Watson and Francis Crick. They created their model using wire and building blocks. This modern model shows a gene, or segment of DNA. The order of the nucleotides contained in the gene (labeled A, T, C, and G) is a code that tells a cell how to produce a certain protein.

So, a gene is a long string of DNA, and the gene's function depends on the sequence of nucleotide bases in the DNA. For scientists researching Huntington's disease, identifying the Huntington gene brought them one very large step closer to understanding the disease.

The Huntington Gene

Our genes are arranged in very precise locations along twenty-three rodlike pairs of chromosomes. One chromosome

CGATTCTGAACATGATACGTACTGGTCCACTAGAACTGAACTCGAGAGGTACTAGA

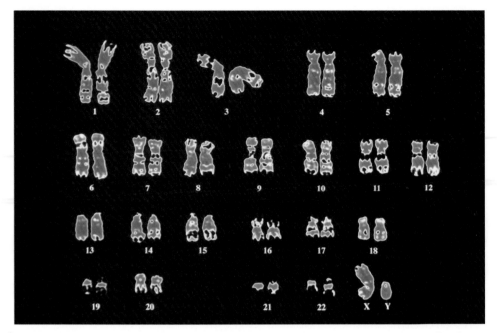

A karyotype is a complete set of all the chromosomes in one cell of an organism. To create a karyotype, the chromosomes are stained with a dye and photographed. Then they are arranged and numbered by size. Karyotypes help scientists identify changes in chromosomes that may indicate a genetic disorder. The X and Y chromosomes at the bottom right corner show that this karyotype is from a male. The karyotype for a female would have two X chromosomes.

from each pair comes from our mother. The other comes from our father. A gene's effect partly depends on whether it is dominant or recessive. A recessive gene will have an effect only if it is present on the chromosomes from both parents. A dominant gene, on the other hand, will always have an effect, even if it is present on only one chromosome. The form of the gene that causes HD is dominant; only one copy of it, inherited from either parent, is necessary to produce the disease.

By gene standards, the Huntington gene is quite long, with more than 300,000 nucleotide base pairs. Sequences of three nucleotide bases are called codons. Each codon is a

DNA instruction telling the cell to produce a certain amino acid. In humans, there are twenty amino acids that link together in a series to make proteins. One of these amino acids, glutamine, is coded for by the codon C-A-G (or CAG). In a normal Huntington gene, there is a section in which the CAG codon is repeated up to thirty times. In a defective Huntington gene, however, the CAG codon repeats more than forty times. This means that for people with HD, there are too many glutamines in the protein produced by the Huntington gene.

The Huntington Gene and the Huntingtin Protein

The protein produced by the Huntington gene, called the huntingtin protein, is present in the nerve cells of all humans. The spelling of the protein, gene, and disease can make things a bit confusing. The protein is spelled "huntingtin"; "Huntington" is the name of the disease and of the gene. Scientists have yet to figure out the exact function of the huntingtin protein, but they do know a lot about it. Huntingtin plays a key role in helping nerve cells function effectively. Scientists also believe that it is necessary for life. In a laboratory, mice that were genetically engineered to lack huntingtin never survived past the embryo stage.

The Structure of Huntingtin

The physical structure of proteins determines how they will function with other parts of the cell. With the huntingtin protein, researchers believe the extra glutamines cause it to have the wrong structure. In people with HD, the defective huntingtin protein is present in cells throughout the body. However, it creates the most problems in the nerve cells of

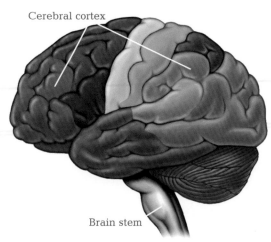

SIDE VIEW OF THE BRAIN

Cerebral cortex

Brain stem

The cerebral cortex is the outer layer of the brain. It consists of nerve cells and the pathways that connect them. Nerve cells in the cerebral cortex send input to the caudate nuclei, deep inside the brain. This information is then processed and relayed to other areas of the brain responsible for controlling complex motor functions. HD affects the cerebral cortex as well as the caudate nuclei.

the basal ganglia, structures deep in the brain that include the two caudate nuclei. Basal ganglia have many important functions, including coordinating movement.

The faulty huntingtin protein also affects the nerve cells in the brain's outer surface. Called the cortex, this part of the brain controls thought, perception, and memory. Huntington's is a degenerative disease, meaning that it causes areas of the brain to deteriorate. As a result, the physical and mental functions controlled by these parts of the brain are affected.

Once researchers understand how faulty proteins affect a cell, they can start to figure out if it is possible to correct the process. This takes many years of research and repeated tests on animal models. But just in the last decade or so, researchers have made huge strides in figuring out a way to solve the HD mystery.

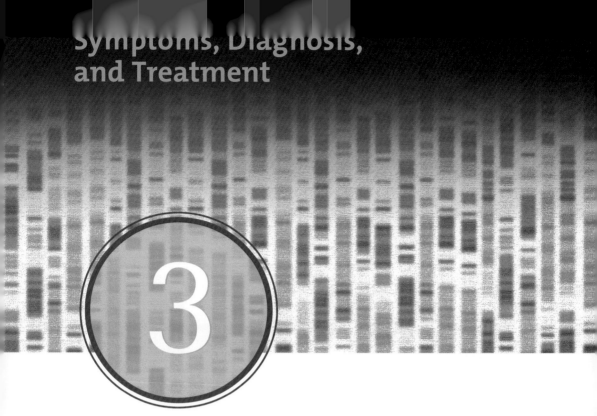

3

We now know that Huntington's is a genetic disease. This means it runs in families. We also know that a person who has a parent with a defective Huntington gene has a 50 percent chance of inheriting the disease.

How do we know this? To start, HD is produced by a single, abnormal gene. Only one copy of the defective gene, inherited from only one parent, is needed to produce symptoms. Each parent has two copies of every chromosome but gives only one copy of each chromosome to a child. This means that a parent with the defective Huntington gene has a 50-50 chance of passing it to his or her child. If the child does not inherit the defective Huntington gene, he or she will not develop the disease and will not pass the gene to his or her own children. But if a person does inherit

TCGATTCTGAACATGATACGTACTGGTCCACTAGAACTGAACTCGAGAGGTACTAGA

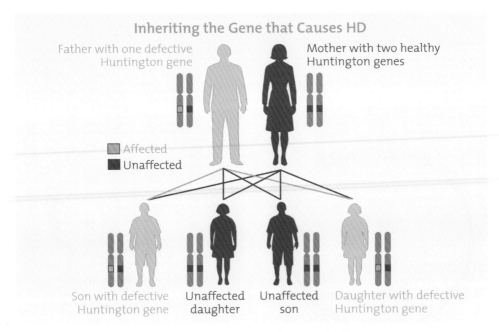

Inheriting the Gene that Causes HD

Father with one defective Huntington gene

Mother with two healthy Huntington genes

Affected
Unaffected

Son with defective Huntington gene

Unaffected daughter

Unaffected son

Daughter with defective Huntington gene

This diagram shows how a father with one defective Huntington gene has a 50 percent chance of passing the gene to a child. There are two types of chromosomes: autosomes and sex chromosomes. HD is an autosomal condition. Since the gene responsible for HD is not located on a sex chromosome, either parent can pass it to both male and female offspring.

the gene and survives long enough, he or she will eventually develop the disease. If this same person has children, each child has a 50-50 chance of inheriting the faulty gene.

What about people who inherit the defective Huntington gene from both parents? This situation is relatively rare, but it does occur. For these people, the symptoms of the disease are only slightly more severe than for people who inherit only one copy of the faulty gene. For those who have two copies of the faulty gene, it is certain that they will pass the gene to their offspring.

When only one parent has the defective gene, having more than one child does not increase or decrease each child's risk. In some families, all the children might inherit the defective version of the Huntington gene. In others, maybe only one child inherits the gene. In still others, maybe no children inherit it.

The Age of Onset

While people with HD can start showing symptoms at any age, most people develop symptoms between the ages of thirty-five and fifty-five. Juvenile HD, also called early-onset HD, begins before the age of twenty. Many believe that the earlier symptoms appear, the faster the disease progresses.

For many people with HD, it is hard to figure out exactly when they began to develop symptoms. This is because the early symptoms of the disease can be very subtle, or not very noticeable. They can also vary widely from one person to the next. Many people may ignore symptoms because the changes are so gradual. For example, people may seem more forgetful than usual or have a slight twitch, but they may attribute this to something other than HD. This often happens if the person does not know he or she carries the faulty Huntington gene. For example, people who are adopted may not know the health history of their birth parents. Or people might not know they are at risk if a parent with HD died before showing symptoms or being diagnosed.

Early Symptoms

The earliest and most common symptoms of both adult-onset and juvenile HD are usually related to mood and result in slight personality changes. For example, a person may seem edgier than usual. Some of these changes, such as increased moodiness and irritability, can be a result of frustration from

JUVENILE HD

Juvenile HD, or early-onset HD, is a form of Huntington's disease that affects children and teens. About 10 percent of people who have HD have this type. The biggest difference between juvenile HD and adult-onset HD is that many children do not experience chorea, a very common symptom of adult-onset HD.

In general, the earlier a person develops juvenile HD, the faster the disease appears to progress. How long each type of HD lasts is not significantly different, but juvenile HD tends to be slightly shorter. Early signs of juvenile HD may go unnoticed. Symptoms include feeling "growing pains" and having more and more trouble with schoolwork. Small changes in handwriting and

These children participated in Dr. Nancy Wexler's HD study in Venezuela. Unfortunately, since the photo was taken, in 1982, some of them have died from HD-related causes. Their participation in the project provided valuable information to Dr. Wexler and her team of researchers.

speech, trouble learning new things, and small problems with movement are also symptoms. Common movement problems include slowness, clumsiness, tremors, or twitching. Children may also become less coordinated or tend to fall more often.

Sometimes diagnosing juvenile HD takes longer because the early symptoms are slightly different from those for adult-onset HD. For example, instead of the dancelike movements (chorea) common in adult HD, movements are stiff and rigid. Seizures are also a symptom in juvenile HD but uncommon in adult-onset HD patients. Also, if the person doesn't know he or she has a parent with HD, doctors may not link the symptoms to such a rare disease.

dealing with other symptoms of the disease and may not actually be clinical symptoms.

Early physical signs include small involuntary movements. These movements may be mistaken for fidgeting during the early stages of the disease. They slowly become more notice-able as the disease progresses. Another early symptom is the loss of interest in personal hygiene. For example, the person may stop bathing, brushing his or her hair, or seeming to care about general appearance. Judgment and memory may also be affected. A person may have trouble driving, learning something new, remembering a fact, answering a question, or making a decision.

As the disease progresses further, other changes become more apparent. It may be harder for the person to concentrate. Trouble keeping balance and "clumsiness" may be more obvious as movement gets harder to control. Depression and mood swings, including anxiety and irritability, may also become more intense.

Many changes in behavior have been linked to HD. These include irritability, temper outbursts, and apathy. Apathy means not seeming to care about anything. HD patients may also seem to act in rude or thoughtless ways. These changes can affect relationships with family members and can cause problems at work.

Middle Stage Symptoms

During the middle stage of the disease, symptoms become more noticeable. Movement problems may make it challenging to do typical household chores, such as washing dishes and folding laundry. Muscle spasms, or uncontrolled movement, in the fingers, feet, face, trunk, and limbs also become more common.

Changes in speech become more obvious. For example, the person suffering from HD may slur his or her words. Some people's speech may become hesitant, or halting. It may also become harder for the person to swallow. As the disease progresses, more nerve cells are destroyed, and patients increasingly lose control of their minds and bodies.

Studies show an increased rate of suicide in families with HD. For some patients, living with severe symptoms of HD—and knowing that HD is fatal—can make life feel unbearable.

Late Stage Symptoms

In the later stages of HD, severe movement disorders are common. These are due to increased neurological damage (damage to nerve cells in the brain). For many people, swallowing and speaking become almost impossible. Weight loss is common. This is a serious risk because it can lead to other health problems or weaken a person's ability to fight off illnesses.

The woman this man is helping is in a later stage of HD. As the disease progresses, it becomes increasingly difficult for patients to control movement. The risk of falling increases, and the person may be unable to walk safely without help. Some patients eventually require wheelchairs because of the inability to balance while standing and walking.

People with adult-onset HD are more likely to experience chorea. For people who develop HD much later in life, the chorea tends to be more intense.

How Is HD Diagnosed?

Thanks to the discovery of the HD gene marker, it is now possible to perform DNA analysis to determine if a person is a carrier of the defective gene. This test is much more accurate than previous methods of testing and requires only a blood sample from the patient. The test can determine if a person has the defective gene before symptoms appear. However, the test cannot predict exactly when a person who has inherited the gene will begin to experience symptoms.

Testing for HD, like testing for any serious disease, involves more than the procedure itself. Usually, testing for HD also involves counseling before and after the test. For

CGATTCTGAACATGATACGTACTGGTCCACTAGAACTGAACTCGAGAGGTACTAGA

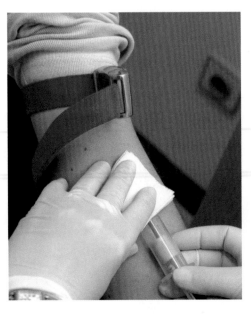

A blood test is used to diagnose Huntington's disease. DNA from cells in the blood is analyzed for the presence of the HD mutation. Blood tests can confirm whether a person will develop the disease. However, tests cannot accurately predict when the person will begin to develop symptoms.

people at risk of HD, deciding to find out if they carry the disease is a big decision. Testing is very personal. Some people decide not to have the test because they are afraid they will change how they live their lives. Others want the test so that they know one way or the other and can make decisions about marriage, having children, their careers, and other long-term decisions.

In general, testing people who are under eighteen years old is not recommended. But exceptions might be made if a child shows symptoms of juvenile HD. Prenatal testing (testing an unborn baby) for the defective gene is also possible.

Treatment for HD

Although there is currently no cure for HD, treatment can help make symptoms less severe. For example, antipsychotic drugs—medications usually used to treat severe mental disorders—may help suppress choreic movements. These same drugs may also

WOODY GUTHRIE (1912–1967)

Woody Guthrie was born on July 14, 1912. He was a popular radio entertainer during the 1930s and 1940s. He became famous for his classic folk songs, including the song "This Land Is Your Land."

Guthrie, shown here playing guitar, suffered from HD for thirteen years. His mother had suffered similar symptoms and died many years earlier. Very little was known about HD then. Before

he was finally diagnosed with HD, Guthrie had been misdiagnosed with alcoholism, schizophrenia, and other disorders. He was placed in many different institutions and hospitals for years before he was finally properly diagnosed.

Woody Guthrie died on October 3, 1967. He was married three times and had a total of eight children. Two of Woody Guthrie's children also died from HD, but his other children are not known to have the disease.

help to reduce the hallucinations, delusions, or violent outbursts sometimes associated with HD. Antidepressant medications can be used to treat depression. For people who experience severe mood swings or anxiety, tranquilizers or lithium may be prescribed. Unfortunately, many drugs used to treat HD symptoms have side effects, including tiredness and restlessness. These side effects can sometimes make it difficult to know if a behavior is a symptom of the disease or a side effect of a medication.

GGATTCTGAACATGATACGTACTGGTCCACTAGAACTGAACTCGAGAGGTACTAGA

The medications used to treat symptoms of Huntington's disease vary widely. Some help with the physical symptoms, while others help with the mental symptoms, such as depression. Medications used to treat Huntington's disease sometimes have harmful side effects. Patients and their families have to weigh the benefits of medications with their possible side effects.

Nutrition also plays a role in treatment for HD. People with HD tend to burn a high number of calories from the constant involuntary movement caused by the disease. Keeping a healthy weight can help reduce involuntary movements and some other symptoms. A high-calorie diet can help people with HD stay at a healthy weight. In addition to maintaining a good diet, patients can learn to cope with symptoms of HD by working with physical, occupational, and speech therapists.

Unfortunately, despite the help an HD patient can receive, there is currently no cure for the disease. Life expectancy from the onset of the disease still ranges from ten to thirty years. Death is usually caused by complications related to HD, including heart failure and pneumonia. But each discovery about the symptoms, the Huntington gene, and how HD functions brings researchers closer to improving treatment and, everyone hopes, finding a cure.

4

Research over the past twenty years has helped scientists gain a better understanding of Huntington's disease. One reason so many advances have been made in recent years is because of the knowledge gained in genetics. Most important was the discovery of the location of the Huntington gene. But the exact function of the Huntington gene is a question researchers continue to struggle with today.

Reversing HD Symptoms

Armed with their knowledge of how defective huntingtin protein causes HD, researchers are

CGATTCTGAACATGATACGTACTGGTCCACTAGAACTGAACTCGAGAGGTACTAGA

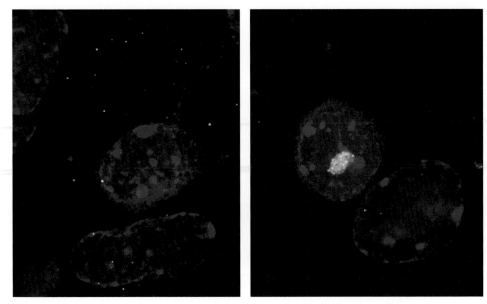

The image on the left shows a neuron in the brain expressing the normal form of the huntingtin protein. The image on the right shows a neuron affected by HD, which produces an abnormal form of the protein. Unlike the normal cell, the HD cell contains an inclusion body, or a collection of abnormal protein. Defective proteins are linked to neuron death, which causes the symptoms of HD.

now asking themselves if the disease is reversible. At the Columbia University College of Physicians and Surgeons, researchers use mouse models to study diseases like HD that lead to the loss or damage of nerve cells. Doctors René Hen and Ai Yamamoto genetically engineered mice so they could experiment with turning a defective Huntington gene on and off. They did this by fusing the defective gene to a promoter that they could regulate. A promoter is a piece of DNA that does not code for a protein. Instead, it controls the expression of a particular gene, in this case, the Huntington gene. They were able to "turn off" the faulty gene by giving the mice a diet that included tetracycline, an antibiotic drug used to treat infections.

When the mice with the inserted gene were given a regular diet, the gene was expressed, and cells produced the defective form of the huntingtin protein. Soon the mice began showing signs of HD. But when tetracycline was added to the diet, the symptoms of HD lessened. This suggests that when the gene was "turned off," the brain was able to cure itself. The movements of the mice improved, as did their memory and overall condition. These results provided the first hope that HD could be reversed.

Another group of researchers, led by Beverly Davidson, of the University of Iowa, also discovered new ways of "turning off" the HD gene and still leaving the normal protein intact and able to function. This process is called RNA (ribonucleic acid) interference, or RNAi. You will read more about RNAi in chapter 5.

 ## Identifying the Onset of Symptoms

Two other long-term studies are also under way. One involves following people who are at risk for HD but who do not know their genetic status and do not plan to have genetic testing. Participants are being evaluated over five years. Researchers conducting the study hope to be able to pinpoint the earliest signs of HD. The other study will follow a group of people who do have the defective gene and know their Huntington status. These participants, too, will be closely monitored for early signs of HD. The goal of these studies is to someday be able to prevent symptoms.

Other Efforts to Find a Cure

These studies are promising, but it is possible that the key to slowing or stopping the disease may be found through other studies. Maybe researchers will figure out how certain brain proteins interact with the huntingtin protein to cause HD symptoms.

A group known as the Huntington Study Group (HSG) was formed in 1993 to conduct basic and clinical research. The HSG is made up of scientists and clinicians from around the world who share information and advances in HD research. They are testing new drugs in the hopes of finding effective treatment for HD.

An organization called Coalition for the Cure was established in 1997 by the Huntington's Disease Society of America, a group of several top laboratories in North America and Europe. Using different types of models, their studies focus on the specific functions of the huntingtin protein and other factors involved in HD. Their efforts all benefit the Huntington Project, which brings together scientists in the field and individuals and families affected by HD.

Previously, it was thought that the age at which a person begins to show signs of HD was determined by the Huntington gene alone. In 2004, however, Nancy Wexler and the United States–Venezuela Collaborative Research Project showed that this was not the case. Instead, the age of onset is strongly influenced by genes other than the Huntington gene, as well as by environmental factors. This discovery implies that there is more than one way to attack HD. Scientists hope that identifying these genes and environmental factors will lead to new treatments and, ultimately, a cure.

Until further developments, current treatment continues to focus on dealing with symptoms of HD, rather than curing

This boy participated in Dr. Nancy Wexler's research project in Venezuela. He was diagnosed with HD at age two. DNA he provided helped lead researchers to the identification of the Huntington gene.

the disease itself. There are many medications that can help to keep symptoms under control, but there are currently no medications that can stop or reverse the disease. However, with recent breakthroughs in research on lab animals, many believe a cure is on the horizon.

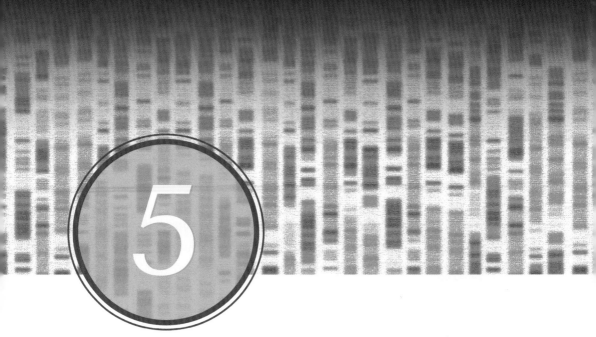

What does the future hold for people with Huntington's disease and other genetic diseases? For those hoping for effective treatment and even a cure, the future looks bright. There are promising studies under way right now, in more than one area. Scientists are looking at gene testing and manipulation, possible medication breakthroughs, and manipulation of molecules in the body. Each successful study brings new hope for the prevention of HD symptoms and a possible cure.

Gene Testing

DNA-based tests, or gene tests, make it possible to test for genetic disorders for several diseases, including HD. One of the best aspects of gene testing is that it can be used to monitor the development of a treatable disease. For example, through gene testing, a person might know he or she is at high risk for developing certain types of cancers. By closely monitoring the patient, cancerous growths can be removed before they become life-threatening.

But gene testing has also been the source of a lot of debates as well. This is because with gene testing, people can now screen embryos for disease. This process is called preimplantation genetic diagnosis (PGD). If a man and a woman decide they want to have a baby, they can provide

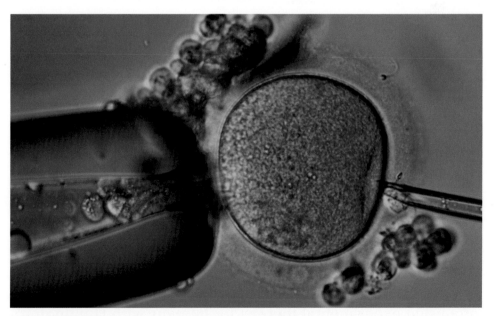

Preimplantation genetic diagnosis (PGD) requires in vitro fertiliza-tion, shown here. With in vitro fertilization, the mother's egg (seen here as a large oval) is removed from her body. It is held under the microscope using a tiny suction (left). The father's sperm is then injected directly into the egg. A glass needle thinner than a human hair (right) is used to inject the sperm.

eggs and sperm to be fertilized using in vitro (outside the woman's body) fertilization. Then, embryos conceived in vitro are analyzed for gene abnormalities that could lead to disorders such as HD. Fertility specialists select only the mutation-free embryos to implant in the mother's uterus. This technique leads to many ethical questions regarding the unused embryos: Should they be donated to science? Is it wrong to destroy them? If they can't be destroyed, should they be kept frozen forever?

Debates over this issue are likely to continue. Nevertheless, PGD is one way parents who carry the defective Huntington gene might be able to have children without passing the gene to them.

Gene Therapy

Using PGD, doctors can increase the chances that an implanted embryo will not have the defective Huntington gene. However, if a child is born with the defective gene, there are some gene therapies that might one day reverse the effects of the disease. There is no gene therapy that actually changes a gene itself. But, fortunately, there are ways of neu-tralizing a defective gene.

You already read about how scientists at Columbia University are able to "turn off" a defective Huntington gene in mouse models. Some researchers now believe the most promising experimental therapy for humans with Huntington's disease is RNA (ribonucleic acid) interference, or RNAi. This is the procedure Beverly Davidson of the University of Iowa helped to develop.

RNAi is different from conventional gene therapy because it specifically targets the defective Huntington gene. Conventional gene therapy works by adding a normal gene.

THE HUMAN GENOME PROJECT

The human genome is all the DNA, or genetic material, in our chromosomes. As you know, DNA is made up of four bases: A, C, G, and T. These are repeated billions of times in the human genome. Scientists knew that understanding the effects of DNA variations could help lead to new ways of diagnosing, treating, and preventing thousands of disorders. So, in 1990, the United States Department of Energy and the National Institutes of Health coordinated the United States Human Genome Project. The purpose of the project was to identify all of the genes in human DNA as well as to determine the sequences of the chemical base pairs that make up human DNA. (The human genome has 3 billion pairs of bases.) Once the information was collected, it was stored in databases and made available to private companies and others in the biotechnology industry. The project was completed in 2003. Scientists can now use this information to carry out innovative research into finding new ways to diagnose, treat, and prevent thousands of disorders, including HD.

Genetic scientists J. Craig Venter (left) and Francis Collins (right) made the cover of Time *magazine on July 3, 2000, for their groundbreaking work on the Human Genome Project. The two men led competing groups that both announced that they had recently completed a rough map of the human genome.*

CGATTCTGAACATGATACGTACTGGTCCACTAGAACTGAACTCGAGAGGTACTAGA

Beverly Davidson studies the effect of RNA interference on RNA levels of the Huntington gene. Davidson's groundbreaking work in gene silencing holds great promise for the development of gene therapies that might one day be able to prevent the neurological damage caused by HD.

It is useful when a disorder is caused by a recessive gene, meaning the affected person has two copies of the disease gene. In conventional therapy, a normal gene is added, and because the normal gene is dominant, it will take over.

However, with HD (and some other genetic disorders), the disease gene is dominant. In this case, conventional gene therapy will not work. As long as the defective Huntington gene exists in the cell, the huntingtin protein will be produced with too many glutamines. This will eventually cause HD symptoms, and it will not matter how many copies of the normal gene are added. The strategy in this situation is to disrupt the expression of the disease gene. RNAi therapy does this.

RNAi suppresses the defective gene but leaves the healthy version of the same gene to carry out its duties. This method, called gene silencing, was the first of its kind to have successful results in the brains of animals, suggesting that it could be appropriate for humans as well. RNAi therapy would be a virtual cure for HD, but there is a major complication: It has been used only in mice that have been genetically engineered to have the defective human Huntington gene. Once the RNAi therapy is performed on the mice, the mutated human protein is no longer produced, and the normal mouse huntingtin protein is left to function correctly. Researchers have yet to find a way to disrupt the defective Huntington gene in humans without also disrupting the function of the normal Huntington gene. We know that normal huntingtin is necessary for brain development. So the next step is for researchers to test how reducing normal huntingtin affects adult animals.

Researchers are also trying to develop RNAi that can be turned off with the antibiotic tetracycline, much like it was done in the mouse models at Columbia University described in chapter 4.

Medicine

The future in medicine as a way to treat HD is also promising. In January 2005, a group of researchers led by David Rubinsztein at Cambridge University in England published results of animal tests they conducted. The tests showed that the drug rapamycin appeared to delay the onset of HD in cell, fly, and mouse models. The medicine was also able to delay the progression of the disease. Until then, rapamycin had been used in patients who received organ transplants. It helps prevent the body from rejecting new organs. But the new study showed that giving rapamycin to animals reduced the levels of the toxic protein that causes HD. The drug worked by speeding up the breakdown of the protein in cells.

While rapamycin is not seen as a cure for HD, it could help delay the disease and allow people living with it to enjoy longer lives. Rapamycin would be meant for long-term use, and most researchers believe that the possible benefits of the medication will outweigh the risks of the side effects, which are mild.

Another medicine that may eventually prove effective in humans is mithramycin. It is a very strong drug normally used in the treatment of certain types of cancers. Researchers have found that mithramycin greatly slows the breakdown of nerve cells in the brains of HD mouse models. This lessens the severity of HD symptoms and allows the mice to live longer. Cells affected by HD lose the ability to produce proteins that are needed for normal cell function. Cells treated with mithramycin, however, seem to continue producing these proteins.

Studies using mithramycin have produced good results. However, much more testing must be done before it can be tried on humans. In addition, there are some negative side effects to its use. For instance, cancer patients using mithramycin often experience stomachaches, nausea, and vomiting. Others have bad skin rashes and severe nosebleeds when using the drug for extended periods.

Rapamycin and mithramycin are two drugs that have shown promise for treating individual aspects of Huntington's disease. However, HD affects numerous functions in nerve cells. Because of this, many researchers believe that Huntington's disease will need to be treated with combinations of drugs.

Molecular Triggers

Another avenue for a future cure for HD involves studying how the abnormal huntingtin protein produced in HD causes the

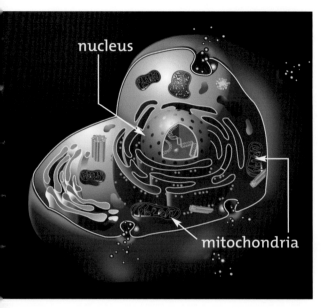

In this image of a simple animal cell, you can see the nucleus in the center. The mitochondria are the bean-shaped structures in the layer outside the nucleus. In cells producing huntingtin, the mitochondria begin to break down. This signals the beginning of cell dysfunction, which leads to the eventual death of the cell.

disease. The abnormal huntingtin protein activates a regulatory protein. This particular regulatory protein is called p53. In turn, p53 switches on other genes. This gene activation is considered abnormal. When abnormal gene activation occurs, it damages mitochondria, which are organelles, or specialized parts, inside a cell. Mitochondria are like a cell's power plant; they are the main energy source of the cell. They also convert nutrients into energy and do other special tasks. When the mitochondria in brain cells don't function properly, the brain cells are damaged.

At the Johns Hopkins University School of Medicine, a study led by Akira Sawa showed that the abnormal huntingtin protein binds to p53 and then increases the level of p53 proteins in cells. In brains of patients with HD, there were substantial increases in the p53 protein. The highest levels were in cases with the most advanced HD.

Researchers found that if they deleted p53, they could prevent damage to neurons in the eyes of fruit flies that had been engineered to have the abnormal huntingtin protein. They then tested the theory in mice. When they removed p53, behavioral abnormalities associated with HD were corrected in the mice.

By figuring out that p53 plays a role in HD, researchers may have found another way to help prevent HD symptoms in humans. Many more tests will have to be conducted before the procedure can be tested in humans. However, researchers are hopeful that by finding a connection between HD and the role of p53, they are closer to finding a possible way to control the progression of HD.

What's Next?

Research for finding a cure for Huntington's disease and treatments for preventing Huntington's disease symptoms are closely linked. But they can be approached in different, and sometimes controversial, ways.

Whenever studies involve gene testing or animal testing, many people have different opinions on the ethical aspects of these studies. Ethics deals with what is "good" or "right." But people's ideas about what types of behavior are ethical can vary greatly. For example, some people believe it is necessary to do scientific research on animals in order to find cures for diseases. They point to the fact that hundreds of diseases have been cured based on animal research. But others believe animal testing is cruel and unnecessary. These people think the negative aspects of the pain, suffering, and death inflicted on the animals far outweigh the potential benefits to humans.

Similarly, people have different views of the ethics of genetic testing. Some people are opposed to in vitro fertilization because not all of the fertilized embryos will be implanted in the mother. Others believe it is wrong to put

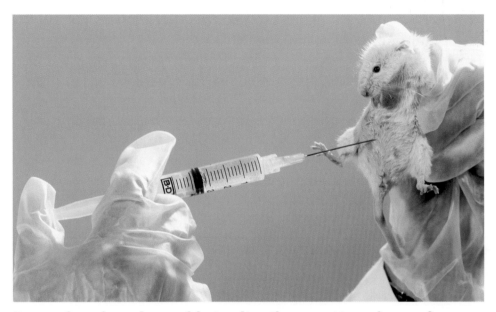

Researchers have been able to alter the genetic makeup of certain mice to have too many CAG repeats. These Huntington's mouse models, as they are called, suffer from the same physical symptoms as humans with the disease. Some therapies initially tested and proven successful in mice are being adapted for future use in humans.

people in a position to choose whether to terminate a pregnancy if they discover an embryo carries a fatal disease.

Like any inherited disease, HD also brings up some difficult choices for people who have it in their families. While the discovery of the Huntington gene has led to major breakthroughs in HD research, it also has made testing for HD much easier for people who have a history of the disease in their families. But testing for HD and knowledge of having the disease raise new questions and concerns. For people who test positive for the defective Huntington gene, deciding to have children and risk passing HD to them can be a very painful choice. Some people choose to take the risk. Others decide to adopt children. Others may decide not to have any children.

For people who already have children when they are diagnosed with HD, other difficult choices lie ahead. For example, should a parent diagnosed with HD tell his or her children that they have a 50 percent chance of having inherited a fatal disease? Should a parent with HD have his or her children tested? If parents know their child has the defective Huntington gene, do they tell him or her? As you can see, advances in testing for HD can bring relief to many, but they also bring up many ethical and moral dilemmas.

These issues are likely to be debated for years to come. In the meantime, research continues, and scientists get closer to finding ways to treat, prevent, and even cure fatal diseases. Families affected by these diseases, including Huntington's disease, have much to hope for and quite possibly not long to wait for a major breakthrough.

The Information Highway

The huge amount of information produced by HD research can be confusing for anyone looking to learn more about the disease. Fortunately for the HD community, the World Wide Web can simplify the search. Through their Web sites, organizations such as the HD Lighthouse, the Huntington's Disease Society of America, and the Huntington's Outreach Project for Education, at Stanford (HOPES) provide access to accurate and up-to-date information about HD. For people who are trying to cope with the disease or think they may be at risk, these organizations also provide information on how to get medical help and counseling.

Other organizations, such as the Huntington's Disease Advocacy Center and the Huntington Study Group, are dedicated to bringing together HD research teams from around the globe. They hope that their networks will make it easier for scientists to share information about break- throughs and medical advances. For people with HD, knowing that these organizations are working together is a source of hope for the future.

Timeline

1500s

The Renaissance physician and alchemist Paracelsus coins the term "chorea" to describe the dancelike movements now known to be symptoms of Huntington's disease.

1630s

English colonists in Massachusetts, Connecticut, and New York begin to describe HD as "that disorder" and "Saint Vitus's dance."

1686

An English doctor named Thomas Sydenham begins classifying different types of chorea and their causes.

1840s

HD is described in medical literature in the United States, England, and Norway.

1872

The landmark paper "On Chorea" is written by George Huntington. He bases his paper on personal accounts of his father's and grandfather's patients.

1910–1911

Researchers begin to note the deterioration of the central region of the brain of HD patients. About this time, they also identify the caudate nucleus as the central target of brain cell death.

Charles B. Davenport, an American eugenicist, writes *Heredity in Relation to Eugenics*. Davenport's study of families with HD is the largest up to that time.

1953

James Watson and Francis Crick discover DNA's structure.

1967

Woody Guthrie, a famous poet and songwriter, dies of HD. His wife, Marjorie Guthrie, founds what is now called the Huntington's Disease Society of America (HDSA).

1976

Joseph T. Coyle develops the first rat model of HD.

Late 1970s

Researchers discover evidence that HD affects cells throughout the body, not just in the brain.

1983

Scientists discover a gene marker linked to HD, which leads to locating the Huntington gene on chromosome 4. The discovery makes it possible to figure out if a person is likely to develop HD.

1993

Scientists more precisely locate the Huntington gene in February. This gene is called IT15 (interesting transcription 15). This discovery makes it possible to determine with even more certainty if a person will develop HD.

1996

Dr. Gillian P. Bates and her colleagues in London, England, create transgenic mouse models for HD research. The mice are genetically engineered to have nerve cell degeneration resembling Huntington's disease.

2003

Scientists involved in the Human Genome Project determine the sequence of all the nucleotides in the human genome.

Glossary

alchemist One who studied the medieval science of transforming base metals, such as iron, into gold.

biotechnology Biological science related to genetic engineering.

caudate nucleus The central target in the brain of brain cell death in patients with HD.

chorea Uncontrollable body movement.

chromosome A bundle of DNA and protein found in the cell nucleus. Except for the sex cells, normal human cells have forty-six chromosomes (twenty-three pairs).

cortex The outer layer of an organ, such as the brain, or other body structure.

degenerative Causing gradual deterioration, or making less healthy over time.

DNA (deoxyribonucleic acid) The chemical structure for genetic material. DNA is made up of four types of nucleic acid: adenine, thymine, cytosine, and guanine (or A, T, C, and G). These are the letters of the genetic code.

ganglia Clusters of neurons located outside the central nervous system.

genetic Determined by genes; inherited.

genome An organism's complete set of DNA.

glutamine A building block of protein. The huntingtin protein contains a series of glutamine building blocks.

hereditary Passed from parent to child through genes.

huntingtin The protein that is coded by the Huntington gene. Normal huntingtin proteins have a repeat series of less than about thirty glutamines. Abnormal huntingtin has more than forty glutamine repeats.

metabolism The chemical changes in living cells related to the production of energy and the assimilation of new material.

neurology The study of the nervous system.

neurons Cells that make up the central nervous system. The human brain is made up of billions of neurons.

nucleic acid Substance found in all living cells where hereditary information is stored.

proteins Chemicals that make up the structure of cells.

For More Information

Healthnet Canada
(Huntington's Disease Page)
24002-621 Fairville Boulevard
Saint John, NB E2M 4X5
Canada
e-mail: info@healthnet.ca
Web site: http://www.healthnet.ca

Hereditary Disease Foundation
1303 Pico Boulevard
Santa Monica, CA 90405
(310) 450-9913
e-mail: cures@hdfoundation.org
Web site: http://www.hdfoundation.org

Huntington's Disease Association
108 Battersea High Street
London, SW11 3HP
England
e-mail: info@hda.org.uk
Web site: http://www.hda.org.uk

Huntington's Disease Society of America
158 West 29th Street, 7th Floor
New York, NY 10001-5300
(800) 345-4372
e-mail: hdsainfo@hdsa.org
Web site: http://www.hdsa.org

Huntington Society of Canada
151 Frederick Street, Suite 400
Kitchener, ON N2H 2M2
Canada
(800) 998-7398
e-mail: sbarnes@hsc-ca.org
Web site: http://www.hsc-ca.org

National Institute of Neurological Disorders and Stroke
NIH Neurological Institute
P.O. Box 5801
Bethesda, MD 20824
(800) 352-9424
Web site: http://www.ninds.nih.gov/disorders/huntington/
    detail_huntington.htm

Web Sites

Due to the changing nature of Internet links, the Rosen
Publishing Group, Inc., has developed an online list of Web
sites related to the subject of this book. This site is updated
regularly. Please use this link to access the list:

http://www.rosenlinks.com/gdd/hudi

For Further Reading

Byczynski, Lynn. *Genetics: Nature's Blueprints*. San Diego, CA: Lucent Books, 1991.

Elliot, Wendy, ed. *Living with Juvenile Huntington's Disease*. Kitchener, ON: Huntington Society of Canada, 1993.

Glimm, Adele. *Gene Hunter: The Story of Neuropsychologist Nancy Wexler*. New York, NY: Franklin Watts, 2005.

Gray, Alison. *Genes and Generations: Living With Huntington's Disease*. Wellington, New Zealand: Wellington Huntington's Disease Assn., 1995.

Gray, Alison. *Huntington's and Me: A Guide for Young People*. Wellington, New Zealand: Wellington Huntington's Disease Association, 2000.

Partridge, Elizabeth. *This Land Was Made for You and Me: The Life and Songs of Woody Guthrie*. New York, NY: Viking, 2002.

Thompson, Michelle Hardt, and Pat Leslie. *Afraid: A Book for Children "At Risk" for Huntington's Disease*. Tempe, AZ: Michelle Hardt Thompson, 2002.

Wexler, Alice. *Mapping Fate: A Memoir of Family, Risk, and Genetic Research*. New York, NY: Random House, 1995.

Bibliography

Arevalo, Jorge. "Woody Guthrie Biography." The Woody
    Guthrie Foundation and Archives. Retrieved August 1,
    2005 (http://www.woodyguthrie.org/biography.htm).

Cha, Jang-Ho J., and Anne B. Young. "Huntington's
    Disease." The American College of Neuropsycho-
    pharmacology. Retrieved August 1, 2005 (http://
    www.acnp.org/g4/gn401000151/ch.html).

CNN.com/Associated Press. "Fifty Year Anniversary of DNA
    Structure Discovery." February 8, 2003. Retrieved August 1,
    2005 (www.cnn.com/2003/TECH/science/02/08/helix.
    anniversary.ap).

Frazin, Natalie. "Silencing Gene Activity Prevents Disease in
    Model for Huntington's." National Institute of Neurological
    Disorders and Stroke. June 7, 2005. Retrieved July 20, 2005.
    (http://accessible.ninds.nih.gov/news_and_events/
    news_articles/news_article_Huntington_RNAi.htm).

Hereditary Disease Foundation. "Hereditary Disease
    Foundation Supports and Catalyzes Critical Achievements
    Toward the Cure." Retrieved August 1, 2005 (http://www.
    hdfoundation.org/PDF/HDF_Achievements.pdf).

Huntington's Disease Association. "New Technique for
    'Switching Off Genes' Could End Fatal Brain Disorders."

January 2005. Retrieved July 20, 2005 (http://
www.hda.org.uk/research/rs035.html).

Huntington's Disease Association. "Transplant Drug Aids
Huntington's." January 2005. Retrieved July 20, 2005
(http://www.hda.org.uk/research/rs032.html).

Huntington's Disease Society of America. "Frequently Asked
Questions about HDSA and HD." March 4, 2005.
Retrieved August 1, 2005 (http://www.hdsa.org/site/
PageServer?pagename=help_info_ed_faq).

Huntington's Disease Society of America. "Molecular
Trigger for Huntington's Disease Found." July 6, 2005.
Retrieved July 20, 2005 (http://www.hdsa.org/site/
PageServer?pagename=news_research_updates).

Huntington's Outreach Project for Education, at Stanford
(HOPES). "The Basics of Huntington's Disease." Retrieved
August 1, 2005 (http://www.stanford.edu/group/hopes/
basics/index/bshome.html).

Huntington Study Group. "Therapeutic Trials." July 2005.
Retrieved August 1, 2005 (http://www.huntington-study-
group.org/THERAPEUTIC%20TRIALS.html).

Kiriakopoulos, Elaine T. "Medical Encyclopedia: Huntington's
Disease." U.S. National Library of Medicine and the
National Institutes of Health. October 23, 2003. Retrieved
August 1, 2005 (www.nlm.nih.gov/medlineplus/ency/
article/00770.htm).

Kolb, Elzy. "Huntington's Disease: Historical and Contemporary
Connections." P & S—College of Physicians and Surgeons
of Columbia University. Winter 2003, pp. 24–29.

Landles, Christian, and Gillian P. Bates. "Huntingtin and the
Molecular Pathogenesis of Huntington's Disease." *Nature*.
Vol. 5, No. 10, August 2004, pp. 958–963. Retrieved
August 2, 2005 (http://www.nature.com/embor/journal/
v5/n10/full/7400250.html).

Mayo Foundation for Medical Education and Research. "Huntington's Disease: Overview." May 11, 2005. Retrieved August 1, 2005 (http://www.mayoclinic.com/invoke.cfm?id=DS00401&dsection=1).

Merz, Beverly. "In Search of Large Families: Kinships That Hold Clues to Disease." Howard Hughes Medical Institute. Retrieved August 1, 2005 (http://www.hhmi.org/genetictrail/b100.html).

National Institute of Neurological Disorders and Stroke. "Huntington's Disease: Hope Through Research." *NIH Publication*, No. 98–90. March 8, 2005. Retrieved August 1, 2005 (http://www.ninds.nih.gov/disorders/huntington/detail_huntington.htm).

Parker, James N., and Philip M. Parker. *The Official Patient's Sourcebook on Huntington's Disease*. San Diego, CA: ICON Group International Inc., 2002.

Partridge, Elizabeth. *This Land Was Made for You and Me: The Life and Songs of Woody Guthrie*. New York, NY: Viking, 2002.

Quarrell, Oliver. *Huntington's Disease: The Facts*. New York, NY: Oxford Medical Publications, 1999.

United States Department of Energy Human Genome Project. "Human Genome Project Information." October 27, 2004. Retrieved August 2, 2005 (http://www. ornl.gov/sci/techresources/Human_Genome/project/about.shtml)

University of Virginia Health System. "Predictive Testing for Huntington's Disease." May 20, 2003. Retrieved August 1, 2005 (http://www.healthsystem.virginia.edu/internet/huntdisease/geninfo.cfm).

Wisconsin Chapter of the Huntington's Disease Society of America. "Facts About Huntington's Disease." May 5, 2004. Retrieved August 1, 2005 (http://www.hdsa-wi.org/facts.htm).

Index

A

animal models, 14, 24, 36, 45, 46, 47–48

B

brain
basal ganglia, 24
caudate nucleus, 10, 24
cortex, 24

C

CAG repeats, 23, 44
chorea, 4–5, 8, 9, 29, 31
Conneally, Michael, 19
Coyle, Joseph T., 14
Crick, James, 10

D

Davidson, Beverly, 37, 42
depression, 6, 16, 29, 33
DNA
and dominant and recessive genes, 22
promoters, 36
structure of, 10–11, 19–21, 43
dopamine, 13

E

ethics, 48–50

G

GABA (gamma-aminobutyric acid), 13
genetic marker, 13, 14, 17, 31
glutamine, 23
Gusella, James, 19
Guthrie, Woody, 33

H

Hen, René, 36
Housman, David, 19
Human Genome Project, 43
huntingtin protein, 23–24, 35, 37, 38, 44, 45, 46–48
Huntington, George, 5
"On Chorea," 9–10, 11, 18
Huntington gene, location of, 14, 19, 35
Huntington's disease
adult onset, 6, 27, 29, 31
and cause of death, 7, 34
early onset/juvenile, 6–7, 27, 28–29, 32

in the Middle Ages, 4–5
names for, 4–5, 8–9, 18
risk factors, 6, 25–27
hygiene, 29

I

inheritance and probability, 25–27
International Centennial
    Symposium on Huntington's
    Disease, 13
in vitro fertilization, 42, 48

K

kainic acid, 14

L

life expectancy, 4, 7, 34

M

memory, 6, 24, 29
Mendel, Gregor, 18
mithramycin, 46
mitochondria, 47

N

nutrition, 34

O

organizations, 50–51
    Coalition for the Cure, 38
    Commission for the Control of
        Huntington's Disease, 14
    Hereditary Disease Foundation,
        12, 13
    Huntington's Disease
        Association, 6
    Huntington Study Group (HSG),
        38, 50

P

Paracelsus, 8, 18
Perry, Thomas L., 13
p53, 47
positron-emission tomography
    (PET), 15
preimplantation genetic diagnosis
    (PGD), 41

R

rapamycin, 45–46
relationships, 30
RNA interference (RNAi), 37,
    42–45
Rubinsztein, David, 45

S

Salem witch trials, 8
Sawa, Akira, 47
statistics, 6, 28
suicide, 30
symptoms, 4, 9–10, 15, 18, 37
    cognitive, 6, 29
    early, 27–29
    emotional, 6, 16, 29
    muscle spasms/movements, 5, 6,
        8, 29, 30, 32, 34
    seizures, 29
    speech problems, 6, 30

T

testing, 6, 31–32, 37, 40–42, 48
treatments, 17
    gene therapy, 42–45
    medications, 16, 32–33, 38, 39, 45

U

United States Congress, 14

V

Venezuela, 12–13, 19
Vitus, Saint, 8

W

Watson, James, 10

Wexler, Nancy, 12–13,
  19, 38
Wexler family, 12–13

Y

Yamamoto, Ai, 36

About the Author

Johanna Knowles has published numerous pamphlets and booklets covering health and social concerns for young adults. She holds a master's degree in children's literature from Simmons College. She won the Society of Children's Book Writers and Illustrators Work-in-Progress Grant for a Young Adult Novel in 2001 and the PEN New England Children's Book Caucus Discovery Award in 2005. She lives in Vermont with her husband and son.

Photo Credits

Cover top © Biophoto Associaters/Photo Reseaarchers, Inc.; cover inset, p. 1 © Jim Wehtie/Photodisc/PunchStock; cover background images: © www.istockphoto.com/Rafal Zdeb (front right), © www.istockphoto.com/ Arnold van Rooij (front middle), © www.istockphoto.com (back middle, back right), © Lawrence Lawry/Photodisc/PunchStock (back left); pp. 5, 9, 10 © United States National Library of Medicine, National Institutes of Health; pp. 11, 24 © 2004 Nucleus Medical Art, Inc. All rights reserved. www.nucleusinc.com; p. 12 courtesy of the Hereditary Disease Foundation; pp. 15, 21 © U.S. Department of Energy Human Genome Program, http://www.ornl.gov/hgmis; p. 16 © Tim Beddow/Photo Researchers, Inc.; p. 20 © Rob & SAS/Corbis; p. 22 © Biophoto Associates/Photo Researchers, Inc.; pp. 28, 39 © Steve Uzzell; p. 31 © Conor Caffrey/Science Photo Library; p. 32 © AJPhoto/Photo Researchers, Inc.; p. 33 ©Library of Congress/Prints and Photographs Online; p. 34 © age fotostock/SuperStock; p. 36 (left and right) © Institut Curie/Frederic Sadou/ISM/Phototake; p. 44 photo courtesy of the University of Iowa; p. 41 © Rawlins, PhD/Custom Medical Stock Photo; p. 43 © Time & Life Pictures/Getty Images; p. 47 © Helene Fournie/ ISM/Phototake; p. 49 © Joe McDonald/Corbis.

Designer: Evelyn Horovicz; Editor: Christopher Roberts
Photo Researcher: Hillary Arnold